Anne Julia is an avid naturalist who has hiked the Appalachian Trail, The Sierra Mountains in California, and the wilds of New England's woods. Her family history dates to the first settlers in Boston, Massachusetts, where her ancestors were part of the *Salem Witch Trials*. She has a bachelor of arts in creative writing from Eckerd College. She lives with her husband, Nicholas, and dogs, Scout and Bruno on the Gulf Coast of Florida.

She Howled is dedicated to my three little birds:

Lilly, Jacqueline, and Hailey.

Anne Julia

SHE HOWLED

Collection of Short Stories

AUSTIN MACAULEY PUBLISHERS™

LONDON • CAMBRIDGE • NEW YORK • SHARJAH

Ordering Information
Quantity sales: Special discounts are available on quantity purchases by corporations, associations, and others. For details, contact the publisher at the address below.

Publisher's Cataloging-in-Publication data
Julia, Anne
She Howled

ISBN 9781649796394 (Paperback)
ISBN 9781649796417 (ePub e-book)

Library of Congress Control Number: 2021925426

www.austinmacauley.com/us

First Published 2022
Austin Macauley Publishers LLC
40 Wall Street, 33rd Floor, Suite 3302
New York, NY 10005
USA

mail-usa@austinmacauley.com
+1 (646) 5125767

I would like to acknowledge that without my husband Nicholas' insistence, this collection of short stories would still be sitting on a shelf, collecting dust. Thank you for the push.

Table of Contents

A Road Inward

Everything is gone from my head, a clean slate, vacant, absent, utterly erased. A vast and arid landscape of nothing, but dry heat and vapors rising. I've searched through its vaulted sandy peaks and its dry cracked riverbeds and find nothing to bring back. All stories of experiences of creative genius have blown out from a massive desert storm in my head. Write something, put pen to your blanched white paper, and form a mark, start with a line, a curve, you can form a word but only if I can find the source that my muse can.

I think that's the problem, thinking too much has brought me here. Perhaps if I trudge back to the sandy sea in my mind and start digging in the numerous banks of my head's ample caches, can I dig up some gold, silver at least? Write I say, spill it out, think of a story to tell, think of a spectacular view to sell, show, and tell all words, describe those sugary places where you can feel the breeze caress your skin on a warm day by the shores of the Cape. Share those tepid feelings you hide behind in dreams, dreams that are lucid with action, running on adrenaline, pumping with fear, or losing or dying for a cause. Become more, create the new; the unheard of before, and do it well.

In this place utter madness reigns, and rains down on me. The air is thick with heat and frustration, I feel smaller and smaller still next to these mountainous sand dunes in my head. I think I am too dim in the headlights of Creative Writers to ever be a cut above the ordinary, but my heart tells me my passion-filled story is just around the next Hill, or over in that Valley over there. Over where though? This desert doesn't have an edge to it, an edge where I can get a good look, peer over and see what I can use for props, yet that's the word that is just as big as this place. Imagination is here, I can feel it.

Out of nothingness, this place conjures up a shovel, it isn't me for certain that creates it, the shovel appears in my hand, it's crimson-pink with a glittery handle. Interesting, something must be growing here, still looks the same around me, all sorts of the color beige, tans, taupe, bleach browns and dull mouse fur looking sand, even I am translucently the color of dried bamboo except for this magnificent pink sparkly shovel in my hand which is now the only marked example of hope in this drab place in my brain. I choose not to dig where I am standing. The ground here is harder than concrete, I walk, no trudge forward on this worn path towards a giant knoll. I have beaten this path here many times before, I can feel that I have, but this is the first time I am armed with a tool, my much-coveted shovel of the word digging hope. I am hoping that maybe I will uncover such great works of a story like an exotic tapestry, all gold with deep reds running through it with bridges to another place and times better than these.

That is where I need to find myself and out of here in this sordid place, which does not move nor change if I lament to stay in this stale place of desolate nothingness. Get to the top of that ridge, that mountain, dig in dirty that beautiful shovel, I know I will scratch it over these rocks, might dent it too. Those are the risks I take to break a little, bend a bit, and dig deeper than I thought I was capable of here in my mind, a place of freedom to be me.

Down East
In Fog and Sea

The clouds sweep in from the Northwest, it looks more like a nor'easter coming through in February, but this is late October. Rolling up and over, then dumping down onto the hills, it blankets the fields below in a fog of blue and grey here in the farthest reaches in the great state of Maine.

As I sit looking out my bedroom window from my cottage that sits at the edge of the Atlantic Ocean in Down-East Maine, Milbridge to be exact, I am elated that I could get myself here, with all its history, deep and colorful; the stories I'll be able to write. The realtor told me my cottage was built by shipbuilders in the mid-1800s, and the bones of it are stronger than any storm the Atlantic could throw at it. My German Shepherd, Scout, paces back and forth behind me, her nails make a slow scraping sound on the bare wood, she lets out a long howl, comes over, and looks out the window with me. "It's just fog, Scout."

How odd, the only time I remember her howling is when an ambulance siren would pass by when we lived in Providence. She is clearly agitated and leaves out of the room; I can hear her careful steps clacking along the floor. She begins howling again, but for what purpose? I like the sound of her primal Wolf side; I follow her out and see that she's at the back door in the kitchen scratching the paint from it with her ample claws and heavy weight.

"OK! OK! Scout, I'll let you... out..."

Lifting the latch, she shoots out through the barely open door, she barks as she exits, she disappears into the fog like a ghost.

I am reminded of an author that I admire, Albert Singer, he was a lover of animals and nature alike.

He said, *" The fear of you, and the dread of you, shall be upon every beast of the earth."* It warms me and comforts me knowing this. Scout is fearless and protective. I couldn't have moved to Maine without her; it was the right choice to transplant my life here in this quiet seaside town of Milbridge. Providence was just too loud, busy, and obnoxious to write a damn thing. Here I am happily alone with all the silence and distance from people, traffic, and politics. I can write all my short stories, novels, poems, and screenplays in peace. I will whittle away at time and life here.

I realize I'm still standing here at the door looking out into the fog and I no longer hear Scout's barking, only a slow hissing sound like a tire deflating. I shut the door; she'll scratch when she wants back in. A cup of tea seems on par with that pressing fog out there. I scan the kitchen, find the kettle, and place it under the faucet, turning on the water, a series of pipes banging, and stuttering and finally dribbling, water flows into the kettle, it's a long slog to fill it. On the glass looking out my window above the sink, there is a circus of flies hammering away at the pane and sill, some belly up in a slow death buzz, too many flies, grabbing a spray bottle of bleach, I fire away with a dome of mist hoping to kill them. Instead of dying, they seem to become angered and attack me, darting at my eyes like missiles. In haste, I shove the window open and make like a crazy woman swatting like I have tennis rackets for hands. They buzz off into the fog that is seeping in as if they were called home. They disappear and the kettle overflows. I drop my tennis racket hand on the faucet spout, and all is quiet again. Save for a high Yip noise that is Scout, I yell out for her, Scout's paws, then her head suddenly appears at the window ledge. I yell, "What the hell!" In her mouth is a lifeless white and brown Seagull. She drops it unapologetically into the sink.

This macabre scene of a dead bird, attacking flies, is too much for me in my logical mind. Scout barks once and is gone in an instant. I slam the window shut and carefully pick up the gull. Its head hanging with tongue and mouth open as if it might scream. The poor bird is wet and still warm, I've never known Scout to kill anything or cause harm. How strange and sad that she would do this. Wrapping the gull in a towel, I place it in an empty moving box that I have left discarded from un-packing in this new home of mine.

I carefully move its head, so it curves into itself at its breast, as if this act is a peaceful gesture to its life before. With my tea long forgotten and my anger boiling up, I decide to go out into the fog and find Scout. I slip my feet into my bright yellow rubber boots and squirm into my matching rain jacket. Throwing open the door with no trepidation, I step out into a cold blanket of fear and fog. I'm immediately aware that I can barely see, looking down

I see my boots through a fine mist of blue. I'm on the shell and stone path that leads to the garden shed, with each step there is a sound of breaking shells. I call for Scout, again and again. I'm met with nothing but silence and a sound of a hiss that went from a tire deflating to the thoughts of snakes on a plane kind of noise. Stop scaring yourself I think! It's just the ocean lapping at the shore, it's just a boat in the harbor using an electric winch to pull up lobster traps. Is there anything else in Down East Maine that has a life of its own that I don't know about? I just haven't lived here long enough to learn its ways, and how people live. As I approach the edge where my shed looms above the cove below, it seems like hours, not minutes till I reach the garden shed. The darkness and fog make it so difficult to see even the outline of this small building. I'm close enough now when I reach out, I find the door slightly ajar. It's hanging by one bottom hinge. I've been meaning to call Tom and ask him to fix it, I'll do it tomorrow for sure this time, I say to myself. The metal handle is ice cold. I open it cautiously as it groans against its one anchored bolt and then it falls quickly off with a hard groan.

Scout jumps out, I fall backwards to the ground, she makes a wild daring leap over me and disappears into the deep mist of blue and gray.

I found this in a book of Stories and Folklore about New England by Lillian Kessler, copyrighted 1941 here's a quote from it.

"There was a famous fabled County never seen by mortal eyes where the pumpkins are growing in the sun and

17

is said to rise, which man does not inhabit neither reptile, bird or beast in this famous fabled County is a way Down East."

Down East

Shipyards Fool

The bellowing blast of the Harbors horn jolts me awake. You'll get used to it, the realtor said, you won't even notice it after a few days, she said. Scout picks up her head, dismisses its sound and drops her head back down on the pillow with a long groaning sigh. She on the other hand has settled in well and is not bothered by the sounds coming from the harbor. I begrudgingly get out of bed and make my way downstairs to make a pot of coffee, have a smoke, and write my next installment to *Down East Magazine*.

The sun is bright and the air crisp. My view of the harbor from my back porch is like a painter's dream. If I had some canvases and brushes instead of a pen, this would be the life to look out into the world instead of down on a blank page. A loud crash breaks me out of my wandering thoughts. Looking over to my right, there is a large stack of lobster traps dividing my property from my neighbors', whom I haven't met yet.

It sounds like empty cans falling pyramid style. "Damn it!" I hear. I jump off my porch and run to the fence trying to peer through and over the traps. I call out, "Are you OK?"

I hear a mumbling and a slight moan of discontent. Scout decides this commotion is too interesting to ignore. She leaves off the porch, runs and jumps up, and rests her front paws on the decaying wooden fence, separating my yard from my neighbors'. She gives a few yips and a deep bark for good measure.

"Can I help you?" I ask. "My name is Bethany Ellis, I moved in here a few weeks ago and I'm your neighbor." I find a narrow slip of space between the cages in the fence. While peering in, I see a small, elderly man splayed out on the ground, crisscross style with rusty cans and a tangle, of course, netting lying on top of him. "Sir, really, I can help you," I call again.

"Miss Ellis, is that your name? That's very nice of you but if you come over here, that Wolf is going to make its way in here too!"

Laughingly, I respond that Scout is a big bunch of kindness, she's harmless. She isn't a Wolf, she's a white German Shepherd. I can see him struggling and visibly tangled, cans clunk and he groans further to himself. "Well, I guess yes, please help me, OK!"

I'm coming over, finding a couple loose fence boards near the end of the lobster crate stacks. I'm afforded a small enough spot to squeeze through the boards and pop off, with these removed, Scout barrels through, of course. I get on my hands and knees and get myself halfway through the fence when I hear the old man shout. "No, go away!"

Then silence.

Once I'm through the fence, I must weave around old fishing garb, lobster traps, buoys and boat parts that look like they have aged with time and the sea's salty kiss. As I approach, Scout is licking the poor man's face. I see him trying to dodge her wet mouth, turning his head side to side.

"Scout, leave him alone, stop," I say.

She does as I ask and sits patiently, next to the man who is trapped underneath these cans and nylon ropes. "Well now you've met my dog, my bit my big bad wolf, are you impressed?"

He laughs a good chuckle. I peered down and into a web of net cans and a friendly face.

"What's your name, sailor?" I ask.

"Emmett Crowley," he says with a smile.

"Well, Mr. Crowley, where to start on this puzzle. You've gotten yourself into a mess."

Little by little I untangle the netting and cans filled with rocks and shells, how odd, soon there is an arm and then a hand free, now he can help himself. Reaching under his shoulders, I help him into a sitting position. I see he is a petite man with short white bristly hair, a leathered face, but with the smiling eyes of the brightest blue. "Thank you, Miss Ellis."

"Call me Bethany. So, what's the story? How do you find yourself all tangled up here?"

"Well, that's a long story, Miss, I mean, Bethany."

He is visibly bruised, a bit scraped, and unsteady on his feet. I help him to his porch, he sits quickly into an anchored swing that hangs precariously from two cabled lines with giant metal hooks. Scout has made her way up and lays down by my feet, sighing heavily as she does. There is a small beat-up red metal cooler next to Emmett. He reaches down, flips the lid, and pulls out a beer. My eyes pop, it's not even noon and he offers me one, and I politely decline.

"How do you like your little house over there," he says, pointing with a crooked finger.

"I like it a lot actually, but it has a few problems with the plumbing and more problems with weird noises and I don't know what causes them; it's got issues."

"It was built by ship builders' way back," Emmett says, "they don't make 'em like that anymore, but you were asking about why I got myself in that bind with the trap I set. Well, I'll tell you, something's been spooking me lately at night and I thought I'd set a trap and catch the little bugger!"

"What do you think it is?"

"Well at first, I thought a weasel or a rabid Coon, but with your Wolf there, I know it's neither."

"Why is that?"

"Cause it's big, real big, something that's not afraid of her in all that howlin' and singing she does."

"Oh! I'm so sorry about that. I didn't realize she is that loud."

"I like her howling and barking. Truth be told I think, it's a shipyard fool, yep, it's been at least fifty or so years now since there has been one about."

"Shipyard fool sounds like a strange thing to me. What kind of animal gets a nickname like that, Emmett?"

"I'll tell ya, one who isn't an animal at all. How long you say you have been in Maine?"

Down East

Wabanaki – People of the Dawn

Orange light bounces on the ocean waves shooting shadows into my eyes as the sun rises over peak foam waves this morning. I step lightly between piles of kelp and crusty cut buoys. I am looking for black stones, all smooth and sleek as dark in a starless night. Scout is with me; she loves this time when I set her free from the confines of our yard and the duty she upholds guarding our cottage. Scout is running up and down the cove with a severed red and white buoy in her jaws, smitten with herself in the joy of being free. I give her less than five minutes before she finds the remnants of a Dead Sea creature and creatively bows down and rolls her nice white fur through it. This will be the highlight of her day to give herself a dip into the odor of fish and sea. I spot a reflecting white sparkle just ahead of Scout frolicking with an old, discarded buoy. I'm drawn to it like a moth to a flame, the closer I get the brighter it becomes, how strange?

Looking down, I see it's a perfectly formed oval rock that is of the clearest white. Bending down to pick it up, my fingers brush the smooth surface that feels like sealskin. I hear a loud howl, I look to where Scout should be and she is gone, so are the piles of kelp and old buoys.

The cove is filled with only rocks and a low tide. I yell for Scout, calling her again and again. I feel confused and displaced, displaced where, and why am I dreaming? The sound of what could only be described as a battle cry snaps my head up. I see out onto the water, two primitive canoe-like boats with two Native American men in each. What is happening, I say to myself and where is Scout? I call for her again, nothing. I see nothing, but the beach before me that I barely recognize.

The canoes are coming closer. I hear them shouting in a language that is indiscernible and getting angrier, the closer they get. I see they are clothed in animal skins and colorful cloths. I tell myself, Bethany, run, but my feet don't move, my legs are planted firm. My mind scrambles to understand what is happening to me, I'm not dreaming, I am here and I'm afraid. The four men jump from their canoes, the tide is out, and their canoes are perched in the flat of mud. They're coming at me with bodies embraced, as if to fight, with a language that spills from their mouths, angry and wild. I cannot move my legs; I Crouch down bending my knees. I see in front of me that beautiful white stone glowing like a pearl at my feet. The men are so close now and coming closer by the second. I reach down and grab the stone, and clutch it tightly, I feel a pulse rip through my hand, up to my arm then, wham! I am spinning in my head, all is black with edges of white.

I See Stars zoom past me, I become still and peaceful, I watch the stars go by my face, my eyes, my hands, in a slow dazzling light show. I hear Scout barking far away as if she is in a space that is not here.

I don't see her here amongst the stars. There is a loud crack as if lightning is here too. I close my eyes, and all is quiet now, too quiet.

Wake up! wake up! I hear from a faraway voice from this nothingness. I begin to feel my feet, my arms, my hands, my head, I feel wetness that is soft and warm over my cheek, I open my eyes and see it is Scout licking my face and Tom, my handyman, is here shaking me.

"Are you OK?" he says.

"What? Why am I on the ground?"

"You got a damn good egg on your head, spot of blood too!"

"I don't know what happened to me, I was picking up rocks and I found this; looking at my clenched hand I open it to watch sand slip through my fingers, where is it?"

I look around, there are no men with canoes on the beach, only piles of kelp and discarded buoys just as they were before. The tide is up, nearly coming in to wetting my boots now.

Tom says, "I think you hit your head pretty hard there."

"Tom, there were Indian men running at me, just over there," I point to the rolling surf breaking on some rocks.

"I think you had a Wabanaki dream there, Miss Ellis. Let's get you home. Scout, you coming?"

Down East
The Vanished Soul

It is said once the spirit leaves the body, it chooses the form it will take next, be it human, animal, or perhaps something else, too. Scout is digging a rather deep hole today off the back porch, dirt flies, claws scraping the sand, shell and rock. Occasionally, she picks her head up to check that I'm still sitting here watching her work. I've wrapped myself up tight in a wool blanket, heavy on my body and soul, I cannot let go of yesterday's events down at the beach. It was real, wasn't it? This large bump on my head should be proof enough. I dreamt it, right? Wabanaki Indians paddling up to shore, yelling, and that rock, that white rock, that was in my hand, right?

Today is the first day in weeks since I've seen the sun, no rain, no fog, it's bliss. I'll take the cold any day, as if on cue with my thoughts, a sharp gust of wind pinches at my face. I pull the blanket up under my chin as armor. I won't go in the house till Scout has finished her excavation dig, and my mind clears. "Miss Ellis!" Emmet Crowley shouts from our fence line.

I am startled by his voice, "Emmet!" looking over I see him standing next to a tall stack of lobster traps at the fence

26

line between our two properties. "Heard you got yourself an egg on your head, how are you feeling?"

"I'm doing okay, thanks for asking, Emmett."

This small town sure has a speedy information highway of current events, I think to myself that was quick. Scout picks up her head and gives Emmet a long stare before going back to her work. She's down deep now, all I can see is her backend, her long white tail, and long dirt plumes launching behind her falling into long piles.

"Miss Ellis, I got to ask, what you think knocked you out cold, down in the Cove yesterday?"

Shaking my head, I answer, "I guess I tripped on a buoy rope, I really don't know, I can't really say."

"I saw Tom down at the docks this morning," he said, "he found you there lying on the beach with high tide nearly at your feet."

I respond back, "Yeah something like that."

"Mind if I come over? Set a bit with you, Miss Ellis?"

"Come on over, there's a couple of loose fence boards down a bit from where you're standing." Emmett lifts a hidden latch, and a fence-like door swings open into Bethany's yard.

"What, there's a door?" I say.

Emmett laughs and walks through, "Yep, it's hinged on my side of the fence. Haven't used it in some twenty odd years or so now."

I am becoming more and more curious about Emmett and his life, his past.

"I can't figure out whether I should be scared or just intrigued by you, Emmet, and Tom too; and all of Milbridge for that matter. Maybe even all of down East Maine!"

Emmet walks past Scout digging away and up the short path through the sunflowers, dead red poppies, and sparse seagrass. He walks up the few steps onto my porch. I notice he is clean-shaven, and his hair is nicely parted to one side, his blue eyes appear quick and kindly. He plops down in a worn thin, but strong, Adirondack chair next to me.

"I'm not feeling too well, not too well at all."

"You'll be fine, Miss Ellis, give yourself a day or two." Emmet peers over and looks me square in the face.

"Well, you don't look too bad, that bump won't even leave a dent when it's done healing!"

I let out a long-overdue laugh that warms me from my toes up.

"I figure it's about time that someone gives you the backstory of your little cottage home, and a bit of history about this part of Maine too, most of it is not all, Whales and Roses, neither, Miss Ellis, Wabanaki Indians is only part of it." Emmet looks down into his hands then looks up to meet my eyes.

"This sounds crazy, but I saw them on the beach yesterday, coming at me out of their canoes, and the beach didn't look at all like it does right now, either! "There's this, Scout vanished! Tom said, it was a Wabanaki dream, but it doesn't feel like a dream at all! I sound insane, Emmett."

Emmet replies, "Near to fifty years ago, there was a young Wabanaki woman that lived here in your little cottage. She was kind, a beauty too. She married a man named Pierre LaMontagne, he came down here from Canada as a boy and grew up not far from here in Machias. He worked the Shipyard and docks as did most men back then. He was known to be the best at any task he put his hands to, lobstering and collecting Sea Urchins to sell to the Uppities down in Portland. He did a bit of snailing, you know, escargot, they like those too. Well, he may have had a strong back and better than most work ethic, but a weak man was he when it came to, Eanna."

Scout gives a loud bark from her hole; I look over to her and away from Emmet. "Come on out of there, that's going to take me a lot of shoveling to put back, Scout!" She ignores my request and continues to dig, only the tops of her ears can be seen now.

"What a beautiful name, Eanna," I say, looking back to Emmett.

"Beautiful she was, but a sad soul, I know she was not a happy woman being married to Pierre. She loved another but was not allowed to be with him or marry him.

"It was a foggy night, much like the night we had a few weeks back. The story goes that she took her life by jumping off the dock, which used to be just beyond your shed there." Emmet points to just beyond Scout, next to the shed. "But I know better, Pierre killed her. Her body was never recovered, even though the Coast Guard and many local divers spent days looking for her. Pierre told a tale of how she ran and jumped right off the dock and into the high tide, and that fog. He said they argued right before she jumped. He was such a mean man before, but after she was gone, he was downright evil."

"Wow, Emmet, that's an incredibly sad story, how does it help me with my memory of yesterday's events?"

Scout begins a long ear-piercing howl. She is sitting at the hole's edge, dirty and exhausted, her neck craned upward for a long, sad, bellow of a cry.

Emmet and Bethany are startled by her, and leave off the porch and quickly make their way over to Scout and the giant hole she has dug. They stand close together and peer down into the ground in disbelief and horror! Scout has uncovered a skeleton, old and beyond decayed but with a shiny-whitestone necklace dangling between a bare rib cage. This could only be the vanished soul, Eanna, who was once lost, but now is found, and will always be remembered.

Fish and the Help

Behind the kitchen line of an old southern restaurant, the walls are dingy, dark, and distressed with years of grime and grease. It is a busy Saturday morning with customers coming and going, hungry for the only breakfast served in town on this small Island of Pass-A-Grille, Florida. The view is picturesque with the Gulf of Mexico in view, with its white-sand beaches, and opulent blue waters set upon the restaurant's front steps. In the dining room there are old wooden tables and chairs, with red and white checkered plastic cloths on each. Kate works here, she is a waitress in her mid-thirties, attractive, small in stature, but a perceptive woman she is.

Kate stumbled upon the job by chance, taking a long walk one day on the beach early one morning as she came to pass the old landmark of this quintessential, seaside restaurant. She jumped at the chance to change her life and vocation, but she is running from her tough past in Boston. Kate is well educated and highly misunderstood by her peers. She finds herself getting caught up in a love triangle of bad proportions and fish problems.

Every morning, fresh fish come in off the docks nearby. Howard Brinkerhoff cleans and filets it by the hundreds of pounds daily. He is a quiet man most of the times, a bit of a closeted eccentric. By looking at him, the phrase "Pelican ugly" comes to mind, but with a deep sense of kindness. Everyone calls him Hoff. He is mean to most, except for Kate. He is known to speak with a deep set of principles of his southern life.

Hoff's claim to fame is that he believes himself to be a self-imposed psychic and believes himself to be a descendant of King Tut. He believes he has lived hundreds of times before now.

There's a breakfast cook, too, Troy DiGiovanni. He is half Cuban and half Italian descent, mid-forties, large in the gut, and smells like a man in need of a shower mixed with old spice aftershave. He is a funny man, with a gentle personality. Troy adores Kate and resents Hoff daily for always trying to lure her in with his tales of fish and psychic predictions, and what he likes to tell her that will happen in her life. Troy does not believe in any of that. "Cockamamie crap," as he puts it. Troy is a man without a dream for himself. He only thinks of Kate, she is his pretend dream when she is working.

Hoff is in the back kitchen filleting fish for the lunch crowd. Troy is behind the line flipping eggs and greasy bacon. Kate is just coming through to pick up her orders out from the kitchen line window. There is a simmering stench of the low tide this morning, coupled with fresh fish, and the delightful smell of cooking bacon.

The perspiration on the steamy August morning fills the room too. The dining room has a chatter of voices and clinking forks clacking against cheap plates that are dinged with age.

Kate is at the line window waiting for her order. "Those eggs done ye?. I've got hungry customers, Troy!" He turns around to face Kate, empty spatula in hand with a look of disdain on his sweaty face.

"Don't you see I've got it coming on, jeez, why are you always giving me a hard time, Kate? I know in five minutes, uses are going to send me through a belt of an order, that I could wrap around my Italian waste, Kate!"

"Troy, I thought you told me you were Cuban too?"

"Eyes' am! Just in my handsome face!" He gives her a wink from his dark eye. Hoff walks into the kitchen, and says, "Are you going to get that breakfast order out to her or what, Troy?"

"What does it look like, Hoff! I'm busy, get yourself back to cutting fish!"

"We've got a lot of people hungry and waiting for your sorry ass to give them something to eat!" Barks Hoff.

"Shut up and go back and cut your damn fish! You got no business out front here, but to be harassing me!"

Kate steps in, "Knock it off, and will somebody give me those eggs frying up in the pan before they're more like hockey pucks than food!"

Hoff gives Kate a childlike grin, turns, and walks out of the kitchen. On his way, he deposits a hefty five-pound box of sausage and bacon onto the counter. "Just thinking you might need this!" It lands with a loud thump! Troy gives Hoff a dismissive look.

A few of the patrons pick up their heads, look up from their coffee and peer over to the kitchen line where Kate, Hoff, and Troy, are standing. The three of them don't notice they're becoming the entertainment for the morning breakfast regulars. Troy hands Kate the plate of eggs she's been waiting for. "Here you go precious, now get those to the tables before they're cold!" He gives her a big smile; Kate gathers the rest of her order and puts it on a large oval tray. She slings it up onto our shoulder like a professional who doesn't know it.

"Thank you, kind sir, I'll be back for that belt of a food order in five minutes, you know!" Kate laughs and reels out with her overflowing tray of breakfast food for the hungry customers who have come for the perfect blue Gulf view and a side of drama dipped in entertainment from the help at the Hurricane Seafood Restaurant.

Part 2
Fish and the Help

There has been a large wedding earlier in the day on the rooftop dining area at the restaurant overlooking the Gulf of Mexico and beaches below. It is now late at night after everyone else has left, except for Kate, Hoff, and Troy. They are in the large kitchen area on the first floor. The Sinks are full of dirty dishes, and many stacks of clean ones are placed about on make-shift tables. Heaping piles of dirty pots and pans are waiting to be cleaned. Setting about are racks of wine glasses that are laying out sparkling against the drab kitchen. Water glasses are laid out to dry on a long stainless-steel table. Without Air conditioning, there is a large ceiling fan set on high. It makes a lovely swishing sound that creates a dull hum in the room.

"Hoff, I could help with those pans?" Kate asks.

"Nope, you just sit right there and relax, just talk to me, I don't need no help." Hoff drops a pan on the floor, it lands with a loud echoing ding.

"See you're getting tired, let me do those for a while."

"Nope, I see you running here and there all day long, never stopping, no wonder you're so skinny, what are you hundred pounds soaking wet?" Hoff gives a little chuckle as if he said something too intimate about her.

Troy says, "Want to mop Kate?" Troy drops the mop into a large bucket which overflows with suds and slops onto the floor.

Kate, "No, thanks, that mop is too big and heavy to push around."

"Troy, you are such a jerk, she's just fine where she is. She's tired, and she needs to rest, damn you are dumber than dirt!"

"Up yours, Hoff, I'm sorry Kate, you sit there and just look pretty and talk to me."

Troy winks at Kate. "She is talking to me, Troy! You just keep slapping that mop around!"

"Stop dancing around each other like prizefighters, please, I'm not impressed at all."

"I've got a new prediction for you Kate. I've seen it in my dreams."

"Ah, Hoff, I don't know, I'm afraid to hear it."

"Well, maybe I won't then, 'cause every time I do, you don't talk to me for three days, Kate."

"I'm sorry, I just couldn't take it, those things you said would happen to me, they did, unfortunately. I can't hear any more predictions, my friend."

Troy says, "Again, damn it, Hoff, leave here be with all of that hocus pocus stuff."

Hoff responds, "Now don't get yourself all Italian-stallion over there, we are just talking, okay, no harm done!"

Troy says, "Just don't be getting her all upset as you did before with all that yakety-yak fortune teller crap."

Kate sighs and says, "He has been right, Troy, so far, everything except the part where I marry him and spend the rest of my life being the wife of a chicken farmer in North Carolina. He has said the truth of things that have happened before it even happened, and I just didn't want it to be true, that's one of the things concerning me and my meandering life. I can't say any more about it."

Hoff smiles and says, "Well, I was just dreaming here, you know that don't you? I do want you to be happy, I won't give you any more life predictions."

Kate smiles back and says, "Thank you, I appreciate that."

Troy says, "Cut it out, just stop all that deep tear-jerking talk! Have you two noticed that it's almost midnight, and there is still work to do before we can leave and go home, to go to sleep, to wake back up, and get back here to open up for breakfast at 6:00 o'clock in the morning.!"

Hoff says, "OK, OK, let's wrap this up." The three co-workers busily finish up their tasks with efficiency and speed. Kate jumps off the counter and starts to help, she smiles as she does, knowing that these two men will always be remembered for the characters that they are and the life lessons they gave.

Hiking North

The train wobbled down the tracks in the summer heat, stuffy air held our anticipation in leaving its safe cocoon of space, confining but comforting at its best. Two well-seasoned and wiry, bearded hikers with bulging calf muscles stood waiting with us for the train to pull up into a stop at Harpers Ferry. A charming and picturesque small West Virginia town is our starting point. This is the unofficial halfway point of the Appalachian Mountains running from Maine to Georgia, all 2,190 miles of it.

"You think they'll make it," says one of the hikers.

"Yeah they'll make it," says the other, waving his hand like it's no big deal.

The train comes to a stop and the doors slide open. Nick and I, unsure of ourselves, jump off and into our first steps. We are so novice we do not know which direction is north and which is south. Forced to ask a local for assistance, "Hey Mac which way is north on the Appalachian Trail?" Without hesitation, the man points over his shoulder with his left thumb.

Feeling like a 12-year-olds heading on an adventure, we walk off following the direction the man pointed to. What we know is the trail is marked six inches by three, white painted blazes on trees, post's rocks, and sometimes on bridges, but as we hike along, frustration replaces our short-lived confidence. I see white markers, but are they the right ones?

"Hey, Julia, how often are we supposed to see these markers?"

"Your guess is as good as mine!"

"Huh!"

"I don't know," I say.

"Are we going the right way?"

"I'm following you."

"Oh no," I say.

"This is your gig, Julia."

"We're in this together," I say.

"Okay, let's just keep walking until we see someone else. We will ask if we are going the right way."

Another 20-minutes pass, "Is that a white blaze Nicky?" I think I see it on a tree.

"Maybe let's keep going, this pack weighs a ton!"

Another mile until we approach a maintenance man with a chainsaw, he confirms what we already suspected; we are going the wrong way.

The frustration turns to inner defeat as our very first steps are a four-mile detour, two miles up, and two miles back.

"Oh no!" says Nick. "West Virginia to Massachusetts, we can't even get past the train station!"

I am the voice of calm reasoning now diffusing the temper tantrum of my trail mate. "Giving up already, it's not even lunchtime!"

"Shit again!" Nick exclaims.

"Alright, quit being so dramatic!" Looking at our guidebook which at that point looked very confusing; nine miles to the first campsite, but nine miles is now thirteen, I am already struggling.

"Come on, Nicky, we are back on track."

We hike down some 200 feet or so and see an actual white blaze!

Nick drops to his knees in some sort of, coming to-Jesus moment at the site of the first real white Appalachian Trail blaze. Yes, we can do this!

The next nine miles pass with exhilaration and a deep feeling of anticipation, mixed with fear. We cross a river on a set of train tracks. What was once flat and easy is no more. We start ascending up a small mountain, it is taxing on our bodies, and our ridiculously heavy backpacks add to our discomfort. Being so focused on ailments and head games, we do not even notice we have now crossed into the state of Maryland. Looking up, I see a rocky and crevassed climb ahead. Above that, I can see an outcropping with other hikers sitting or standing at its edge.

"Look up, Nicky!" I say.

I see his head pop up, he asks, "How are we going to get up there?"

"On our two feet, use your hands if you have to!"

With much foot and handwork, we crawl up and onto the ledge, it is a vast vista of open views of the Potomac River below and West Virginia is behind it.

Hazy with low clouds, all colors of burnt smoke, and sunshine, we drop our packs and feel elated at our achievement and the reward of this satisfying view. We languished here for some time. The sun has begun to set. I think to myself scary thoughts of what the night will bring of bears afoot, possibly rattlesnakes slithering by our tent. I need to push these thoughts out of my mind, soldier on, and settle into this new routine of hiking as many miles as we can, set up camp, eat, then try to sleep with the animals just a thin veil away from our beating hearts inside the tent. "Let's go," says Nick, interrupting my disturbing thoughts. We lift our packs clumsily, put them on our aching backs, buckles, and straps click here and there, readjustments are made to its bulky fitting. Am I wearing this right? The straps are digging into my shoulders. I feel like I am going to tip backward with one misstep. I need help, but I keep myself silent, sulking in my discontent in order not to damage my pride.

Another two miles through a meandering hilltop thick with underbrush and dense trees, we come to our very first shelter area; a three-sided, open-air structure. There is a large fire pit and a dilapidated picnic table with lots of Hikers lazing about talking in pairs or small groups.

Tents of all colors, green and orange, canvassing the shelter area are set up in a somewhat lightly wooded area. Some Hikers have set up inside the shelter with sleeping bags rolled out onto the floor.

We find a narrow slip of untouched ground on a slight slant, and decide that this must be our allotted space, we then begin the painstakingly difficult process to assemble our green two man-tent. It should have taken under three minutes as we had practiced putting it up and taking it down before we had left our safe harbor of home. But here it's turning into a fight; and an embarrassing one at that! Twenty minutes or so later our little home was created.

Seriously, are we going to make it? We must be nuts to try living outside and walk hundreds of miles through many states north. How about back to the train station? How about back to the real world?

Nick says, "We need water we are out."

"Can't be!" I exclaim.

He replies, "And you are the one who drank most of it!"

It's time to learn how to collect and clean water to sustain ourselves. We know by our trusty Appalachian Trail guidebook that there is a water source close by. I tell Nick, "You can ask one of those Hikers over there?" pointing to the shelter area.

"Eh, you do it," he says.

"Nope, you. I am going to figure out this gas cook pot and make us something to eat."

Nick quickly grabs the empty bottle and the sawyer pump system too. He huffs out and over to the group of hikers. I see him chatting for a few minutes with them and then he disappears into a thickly treed area out of my view. My heart pounds instantly. I feel unsafe and insecure, I count the minutes till I see him pop up, and through the woods, he looks sweaty and has a slight limp.

"Oh my god, that was really far down this mountain!" He drops the bottles of water to the ground.

He also drops to the ground! I say, "Are you alright?"

Nick replies, "Next time you're getting the water!"

"Fine, I will, it couldn't have been that bad?"

"One step above hell is what I would say about that water run. I did see two deer up the stream just watching me filter the water. That was the best part."

I finished making our very first meal in the mini propane cookpot. It was a Mountain house variety brand of dehydrated Beef stew, coveted by hikers and truly an expense we liked to indulge in occasionally. This attempt of mine to cook it into a soup version was barely edible and quite an unpalatable meal, I was banned from cooking from then on out, really, though I was very happy to be relieved of its duties.

With our dinner complete, we followed that up with a near flavorless granola bar for dessert.

It is now time to hang the food bag on a far-reaching and very high tree branch.

There is a first time for everything, and this event of nightly ritual would prove to be a challenge, I beg off this responsibility too. Nick has an incredible pitching arm and aims; how hard could it be?

Nick ties a rope to a small pocketknife and makes several attempts to launch it over a nearby branch about forty feet high. Each try it misses its mark and is a buck short.

Lumbering nearby is a large man who looks like a cross between Benjamin Franklin and an ageing Rock Star, he says to Nick. "How ya doin? I don't want to be that guy, but I got to be that guy!" Nick looks over to him and shrugs his shoulders too exhausted to respond.

"You need a branch further out and higher to keep the Bears from snatching it!" says the older hiker who absolutley looks like an aging Rock Star to me. Nick looks out into the woods with its low shrubs and darkening forest. "I'm not going out there with the rattlesnakes. This is the tree!"

43

"You're doing great!" exclaims the man. The next pitch Nick nails the shot with the rope going over the branch. Immediate cheers go up!

The older hiker and Nick share a high-five. Goodnights are exchanged and a new friendship is just beginning too. I think to myself, what animals will creep around the tent tonight, and will I wake to the morning light.

Five Day Rule
Hiking North

Every little sound of a twig snapping last night, I was sure there would be a bear ready to piñata our tent to shreds; with us the prize of fat candy inside. This morning, our bodies ache and there are pains not before felt. My question again is if we can do this or not?

Upon the Ridge, casting a nice glow of sunshine down on our campsite. We find a renewed sense of adventure. A determination runs through us now that we've made it through the night. Nick is already busy dissembling our camp area. Struggling trying to deflate my air mattress, it hisses and squeaks as he attempts to make it smaller so that it will fit in my pack. We then double-check our area to make sure we have everything before we buckle our straps and hike. Nick takes a verbal inventory that will become routine. "Ok, Audrey," he says to me. "Got everything? Poles? Wallets? Phones? Smokes? Lighters etc. Cuz once we walk forward, we're not coming back!"

With a late Nine AM start, we're about an hour behind the other hikers. But one of the nice things about The Appalachian Trail is that there is no schedule, and you hike your own hike. We set off for a ten-mile day, which unbeknownst to us, is a cakewalk compared to the 20-25 mile stretches the thru-hikers manage. Walking in wonderment through rhododendron bushes and pine trees, we share the thought that there can be no place like this on Earth. We are so happy to be here. We scurry down a ridge about two miles and descend into Gathland State Park in Maryland. We will pass through many of these small parks North, many of them also being historical Civil War battlegrounds. We come to a nice mowed area with benches here and there, we also find two other hikers here, Ted and Jo, a husband and wife, who have hiked every summer for the past several years, some two to three hundred miles or so each time. They are more than halfway finished with their hike at this point. The trail is over two thousand miles long to walk. Ted happens to be the man Nick met last night during the "bear bag incident." Both Ted and Jo are kind and incredibly knowledgeable about hiking. They are experts, I would say with gear, food, and what you should, or should not be carrying in your backpack. If not for meeting them on the second day of our hike North on the Appalachian Trail, we most likely would have marched back to Harpers Ferry and jumped on the next train to D.C.

The chance meeting and befriending Ted and Jo would be a game-changer for us. Feeling the need for a break, we dump our packs and flop down onto an old wooden bench. Ted strikes up a conversation with us about the next 30 miles ahead of us, and its significance in history; the battles that were fought here between the North and the South, and the monuments we might see along the way. He says, "If we look closely enough to some of the stone walls, we might just spot a long-forgotten gravesite of Confederate soldiers buried in haste during the deadly battles that afforded these lush green lands and their place in America's history of freedom." We decide to confide in our newfound friends that we are novices and unsure of what we are doing, and if what we are doing is right? One of the biggest complaints we have is our backpacks, they just don't feel right. Are they supposed to feel this way? Are they too heavy? They're digging in at the shoulders and sides. Nick is getting blisters and red marks on his hips that hurt him terribly. Ted says, "We should do a shakedown, dump everything out of your packs, and see what you got in there that's not essential for living outside and walking every day!" Ted first makes some adjustments to the straps on the side of Nick's pack and to the mainframe itself, shortening it making for a better fit and carry. Now that our contents are splayed out on the ground, it's determined that both of our packs need serious adjustments made to the many unnecessary, heavy items we are carrying. "These are the things you don't need, an Arctic sleeping bag! In June!" Ted gives a deep laugh, then continues to explain what else we do not need to carry. "Two pairs of running shoes, that's a no."

Too many shirts, shorts, socks, books, a deck of cards, nope! Seriously, what were we thinking? We would be able to send these items back home sometime later, that is if we truly and earnestly hike on. I am honest with myself and Nick for the first time about my confidence to hike on. "Maybe we made a mistake? Maybe we should go home?" Ted says this, "Jo and I abide by the Five-day rule. Don't give up until you've been out for at least five days." We both find Ted's words comforting as well as permission to

47

be in the moment in the woods without the pressure of failure.

Ted's wife Jo adds, "You guys can do this! You can tag along with us if you like and learn the ropes, ask as many questions as you want."

"That would be awesome," I say. I give a smile and a reassuring nod to Nick. We pack up and shove off onto the white blazed Trail ahead. The next few days pass with easier terrain and well-slept nights. The Maryland section of the A.T. is filled with historic Civil War Monuments and battlefields.

From a rocky ridge, we look down onto an expansive valley where the battle of Antietam took place. Nick being a bit of a history enthusiast shares his excitement and knowledge of the bloodiest battle of the Civil War with me. "You can almost imagine the soldiers and cannon fire," He exclaims. "The generals stood right here and commanded the troops," He adds.

"Ok let's go," I say. Nick drops his hands in frustration after seeing my unexcited response. We ask endless questions of Ted and Jo and they happily volley answers back that help us hike smarter, and stronger too. Showing us that we can make it to the Mason Dixon Line. Pennsylvania here we come!

In the Kitchen with Nancy

The smell of lemon and spices filled the kitchen on a cold spring day up in the hills where I lived in a home built with logs. Nancy, my stepmother, has a gift for creating amazing tasting cuisine for us to eat. The taste of which only memory serves me now. Nancy, my stepmother, has a gift, but a far greater person is she who gave us years of delicious food to eat every day. She is the lifeblood of the family.

Today, my father has brought home four Rainbow Trout from his fishing trip at Lake Champlain. This is the arrangement, he catches them, I gut and clean them, then lay them out in a formative row on the counter, then Nancy cooks them. This routine will play out over the years with more Trout of the kinds, which are Rainbow, Brook, Lake, and an occasional largemouth Bass too. Perch may be delicious to eat, but too many bones to be practical. Eating well and in a health-minded way is Nancy's daily gift to us. She often spends hours in the kitchen creating meals for us.

There is chopping, mixing, measuring being performed all in the background of our log cabin, but seemingly the most important, if it was my father who was to be in charge of this life-giving necessity, my brothers and I would have starved, or sustained solely on peanut butter and fluff sandwiches, which he was known to make.

I like to hang out in the kitchen with Nancy, I watch her in awe of the tasty recipes she creates, oh and the heavenly cookies she can make. God help us all, they are amazing! You can't have just one or two, more must be consumed, so one can feel the peaks and saturation of the sugar and butter flavors dancing on the tongue.

There are times if I'm not watching her cook, I am nearby in Nancy's pantry. There would rest the vacuum cleaner, assorted brooms, and cleaning supplies, a tower of shelves of canned goods, bags of potatoes, onions, and vast stores of her cooking implements too. Here I sit on the vacuum cleaner and contemplate my future. At times, this pantry is my time machine that I created to take me anywhere, and any place I like to go, such as the lands of Yoda in the Empire Strikes Back movie, or to the next year and imagine myself swimming in the Gulf of Mexico with dolphins, and sometimes back in time too, to relive a sadness I want to keep close, but today I'm making Nancy a menu of sorts. I have written down every item in her pantry. It takes me such a long time and when I'm almost finished, she calls me out of the pantry; my time machine, because supper is ready! I hand her my list of pantry items. I have conveniently crafted into a menu, complete with cover, title, and folded pages. Then she hands me perfectly cooked and seasoned Rainbow Trout cuisine.

Love & The Sea

I walk along a pebbled path to the Sea, sand at my feet, wind, and sun on my face, alone I venture on seeking to find the love I feel in my beloved. Solace gives way to feeling free, to let go of him. Life is hard, suffering is expected, but love is the only path I choose. Once we were young, wild, and free, a Beauty Queen and a Bar Room Singer. We look great together, the invincibility of youth and the confidence of Nobles gave reason to merge with one another souls. My hair ringlets of gold that flowed like a Persian carpet caressing my youthful skin with kaleidoscope eyes, and he emulated all handsome maleness from every essence of his being, with a voice, a voice in song that stills the heart and captivates my soul. Forward into the heart, we played and danced like children, we fought and felt like samurais, wholly living in each other's moments of the young at heart. When time aged us, I changed, beauty faded, and my mind became my triumph. When he changed, demons rushed in, took over, and left me for bones, vultures even passed over.

In the meantime, I remembered this, it's a real-world pleasure feeling, the rush of adrenaline coursing through my veins, just from one look from him was intoxicating. Oh how I lived in those moments that carried me through to here. I look down now I see waves crashing on emeraldgreen rocks, smooth with age from timeless motion, always moving in and back. I step gently, for here is where I crossover to understand my loss and stay dry. Is it true that the love of the beloved can break us if left unattended like a dry garden? Yes, but I soldier on and believe I was not betrayed by him, but by my own devotion to him. I felt my own suffering for his way of life, which consisted of booze, lies, and pretty women. This I believe, I felt my heart mend, the suffering had ceased when I finally understood its purpose, to make me more, make me whole again. Now the edge of the sea before me, cloudy, stormy skies above, I hear his song, he sings to me, his lover, hold still your heart, please don't move on, I can see the path to the Sea, I will meet you there, I will be better, become more, more for you, my beautiful Queen, my most beloved one. This I believe, love sees no evil, it does not discriminate overtime, it only sees what it wants you to feel, and it wants you to feel love in your heart. Forgiving myself was the answer and letting go of him was just the beginning of a whole new world for me.

My Life Jacket

Little round stones lay on silt and sand canvassing Lake Champlain's shoreline. It was July and my world smelled of fresh air boosted in on a strong wind. The lake is my childhood playground and always has better memories than most, with some years later sulking off in broken promises and dreams not lived. Here on the lake is where happiness lives. Uncle Pete and I had so much fun building sandcastles in my skies and stone houses made of clay buttons in his. Uncle Pete, a tall dark-haired and blue-eyed always smiling man had a way with his words and away with life. He always chose the, "let me tell you a joke or let me teach you how to swim," approach to my life. I am a puny and capriciously small-statured girl with curly blonde hair and alabaster skin. But with my attitude, I stand tall. I am an open book for those who can read me well, Uncle Pete is one of those readers.

Uncle Pete is taking out the rowboat, and of course I want to go, but Marge, my grandmother, thinks differently.

"You're not going in that boat without a life jacket on," says Grandma.

"Yes, I am going," I reply.

"Nope!" she says.

"I am not wearing that ugly life jacket!"

"You're wearing it or you're not going!" she exclaims.

"Uncle Pete is not wearing one!" I yell.

"He is twenty-three years old, and you are five, you're wearing one!"

"I won't!"

"No, Julia, you're not going in that boat unless you put that life jacket on!"

"Uncle Pete has taught me to swim. I don't need a life jacket!"

Uncle Pete pleads with my grandmother to let me go with him as he sits in his rowboat bobbing up and down as little ripples of shore waves roll in after a motorboat passes some distance behind him.

With a firm and there will be no more discussion about it! Grandma ends it with "No you will not get in that boat; this conversation is over, Julia."

Uncle Pete and I drop our heads and slump our shoulders. We look as if we are bowing to the almighty matriarch of our family, she has won, yet again another round of keeping her only grandchild safe in her mind. Tears sting my eyes for a moment, while my anger boils up to a full froth. Like a volcano, I erupt with foul language that spills out of my mouth, not from a 5-year-old, but a matured inebriated Irish sailor instead. These expletives lead me wildly out of control, yelling and running down the lake's edge and up the wooden stairs that lead to our cabin perched above it. If only I had known then, that anger is the energy of fools. Uncle Pete is my favorite person in the whole world. I feel so happy around him he makes me laugh and I love him for it. I stop at the top of the stairs and watch him row away, I shout, "Uncle Pete!" My voice is a pathetic arch of sound reverberating out of my mouth. It makes my throat tight; it hurts me, I am in pain due the separation from him. I know now if I had put that ugly life jacket on, I would be with him gloriously sailing off to mysterious small islands to explore nearby. Oh, the adventures I missed because of my stubbornness. The idealism I held so closely to my identity keeps me right here looking out at him rowing away and into his own future.

Hours pass as I sit waiting for his return, I watch the birds fly over the lake, an Osprey here and there, one dives in for a fish for their supper. The sun dips behind the mountains beyond the lake, dragonflies start their dance on the water, they appear to bounce and glide on it, I find it very calming to watch, and pass the time as I wait for my favorite person to return. Down below me on the beach, my grandfather is building a fire in the open pit BBQ; he has gathered vast amounts of dry driftwood and a few pieces of oak logs for good measure. Approaching me, I hear a chorus of sing-song voices. It is my grandmother and her sisters, Ginny, and Marilla. They step by me with ease and descend the wooden stairs each carrying a large bowl or pot and grocery bags stuffed with ears of sweet corn, grown from the nearby Addison fields.

I hope there's dessert is the first real thought I've had since the INCIDENT earlier. I pop myself down a few steps, sit again and try to peer over and listen in on the talk I hear brewing from the family below.

"Marge, where's Peter?" asks Marilla.

"Oh, he'll be back soon I hope." She responds and peers over in my direction.

She sees me staring at her as I am the Bull, and she is the matador. Grandma looks away first and continues busily to help her sisters set up tonight's supper by the lake.

The fire is nicely ablaze now. Aunt Ginny hands grandpa ears of corn to put on the wire grill he has placed over the fire, he lines up the ears of corn in a tight formation.

I hope it's sweet. I love sweet things; I say aloud to know one.

I bounce up quickly and head down the rest of the steps and slip down to the water's edge. The beach is covered with little flat stones made of clay, really, they look more like buttons, how odd. I find a nice thin and flat one, power up my arm, and sling it off over the water. It ricochets once off the top and sinks on its next leap. A pinch of perfection raises up in me. I bend over for another stone, just then Uncle Pete's tennis shoes step next to my hand, they're worn heavy with clumping mud and clay about them. I look up into his face which is shadowed by the setting sun, it gives him an appearance of a haloed angel.

"Did you miss me?" He asks.

I smile and scan the shoreline.

"Where's the boat?"

Uncle Pete says, "It's over in the next cove!"

I stand up straight, rock in hand "I'm glad you're back, I've had problems with Marge!"

"You really should call her grandma you know."

Uncle Pete shifts his tall and seemingly gigantic body slightly which reveals a blonde haired, slender, attractive girl talking about with my Aunts.

I am instantly aware of the possibility of an intruder into my tight-knit family.

"Who is that?"

My eyes squinted with instant disdain.

"That's Jackie," he says.

"Why?"

"Why what?"

"Why is she here?"

"I invited her, and she is very nice. I think you might like her, Julia."

"Ha, I doubt it!"

"Give her a chance, do it for me, please."

I let out a long sigh and grip the rock in my hand tighter. I say, "OK, I'll try."

"Come with me, I'll introduce you."

I drop the rock in my hand, it lands with soft tink onto another rock below, Uncle Pete picks it up and launches it out onto the top of the water. It hops and skips along like one of those dragonflies. We watch it go out so far, I never see it sink. He is magic Uncle Pete, everything about him is, he holds all my love, his patience teaches me to trust; my life lessons revealed to me that to remember him is to always keep loving him.

The Light at Templeton

It is a dreary and foreboding night as I look out my window
beyond the barns and into the Apple Orchard where the
wind whips through its barren branches. There are a few
apples that swing dead, clinging to a tethered afterlife. This
is my view here, my whole world now at this old Inn, in
Templeton Vermont. I've heard from its townsfolk that
these Hamlets can stay in a funk of gray for weeks, even
months at a time. How could I not sulk by these weathered
hills? This old building creaks and groans when the winter
blows in; it cries in the night, I hear it. This Inn has been
open for as far back as the Revolutionary War and used as
a field hospital during the battles that were fought near Fort
Ticonderoga. I've heard frightening tales of hooded figures
and whispered stories of unnatural events that have
happened here over centuries into decades, albeit to give an
unwelcome gesture to anyone who might think to settle here
in this Hilltown.

I have come to stay only because my mother left me
here for Middlebury for work, for a short while she said, but
I know better. I look over at a picture of Uncle Pete on my
bedside table. I like to look at it and remember him. He's
leaning against an Apple tree out in the Orchard. It has

faded to a mustard-colored hue that makes him look old, but he was so young.

My rumination is interrupted by a loud thump at my bedroom door. "Time for supper, Marrila!" Aunt Leora shouts.

"I'll be down shortly!" I reply.

That woman is by far like a tack in my shoe, hard-pressed and difficult to remove; if it weren't for her, I do not believe I would be here. I've spent seven months and thirteen days wandering about this old place with its stench of Maple and Oak smoke from the woodstoves burning overwinters into damp Springs. How long do I have to wait, how long till I can move away, how long?

Down in the kitchen, Leora sits frumpily in her worn thin Windsor chair with her fingers thrumming the armrest like a drummer at taps. I sit down gingerly on the opposite side of the table. Leora sails right into a hateful yarn of how Mr. Crompton, the caretaker, is trying to destroy her inn. "Marrila, I found a piece of my grandmother's old quilt in the back garden wedged under a fieldstone; I know it was him! He's not going to get the best of me! I'll tell ya!" Leora swipes a piece of black greasy hair that falls across her forehead. She grins and bares two crooked teeth jutting out from her bottom lip. I push my chair back a few inches to distance myself from her foul and rotted breath. I hurriedly eat my barely warm fried potatoes and ham. I choke it down, swallow hard, make my excuses to leave, and scurry to the solace of my room.

The sound of steam radiators knocking, and hissing is all that I hear settling in on this cold night to come and to come to pass by the morning light. I look out my window

59

and I see the sunlight is growing dim as the sun sets behind the Orchard and the Hill it rests upon. I watch the light play on the Apple trees with the wind picking up, it looks menacing, as they dance and bend like swords about to strike. Out of the corner of my eye, I notice a hunched figure slowly walking towards the barns; it's too small to be Mr. Crompton, that man is the size of a bear. Perhaps a wayward guest is looking for a room to let.

I throw open the window and shout, "Hello There! if you're looking for a room, the Inn is over here!"

The figure quickly disappears behind a bulky roll of hay left by the barn door. The evening light is fading into night, dark and quiet. There aren't even any stars, only a sliver of moon hangs down beside the silo. I don't think he heard me.

I call out again, "If you need a room come this way!" Nothing but silence.

I am becoming very afraid. I call out for Leora. I call out for her again and again! I call her as I run out of my room, "Leora!" I sweep through the house yelling for her as I make my way to the first floor. I hear a thundering crash like splintering wood, then a scream which sends shivers down my spine. I run down the hall and descend the narrow steps which lead me to the kitchen. The only light I see is a warm glow of orange from the wood-burning cook stove. I smell a sweetness that fills my body with delight and relaxation. Apple, blueberry, pear, and tart blackberries with the smell of cinnamon are intoxicating. I should be scared, no, terrified, but oddly I'm not. I feel warm and safe like the summer months I spent by the Lake in Addison. My odd trance is broken by Leora who is standing in the corner shadows staring at me like an Osprey, and I am the fish.

"Come, child, follow me." And I do. She reaches for the knob of the root cellar door; a place I've always feared to go. The small wooden door slowly opens, it groans against its hinges and opens with a pop! A metal railing glitters white and sparkles like green jewels when I peer in. Looking down, I see a bulky figure emanating a green glow at the bottom of the rusty iron steps. Before I can get the words from my mouth to stop her, Leora sweeps down the steps and disappears somewhere beyond the glowing figure. I stand at the top, my foot poised to make my first step.

In the shadows, a light bulb swings back and forth from its cabled line above my head and begins to become bright, and brighter still, curls of smoke seep out from its silver coil, sparks fly and snap! I want to turn back now, but I stand here resolute with my legs as planted as a rooted tree, my arms unarmored without a weapon in hand. I close my eyes to shut out the light and think of days better than these.

The Mountain and the Mare

The fall air is crisp and cold and smells of overripe apples fermenting on heaped piles from barren trees spilling like honey onto the frosted ground on this dry and sunny day in October of 1978. In a small New England town up in the hills and far away from the cities that exist out beyond the pine trees, and far away from the Valley below.

The rumbling yellow school bus rounds the bend creaking on its old frame, bumping over rocks and small stones on this dirt road. I stand waiting, clad in my oversized red jacket, and blue jeans today. I've forgotten to take off my farm boots and replace them with my school shoes, but here I stand waiting. I see it coming now and it lurches down the steep hill with brakes that squeak and grind as it comes rattling to a halt just a few feet in front of me. The bus driver pulls a lever; the doors fold open with a slow hiss then a snap! I jump on, hurriedly, and take a seat. I'm alone here, save for the bus driver who is having her morning smoke as she drives. My fellow students have the option to either get on the bus before picking me up in what is now known as Morin Hollow, or the very bottom of the mountain, or they can wait till the old yellow bus has already picked me up.

Today, I'm alone as the other students picked the latter. The bus rolls down the road, past my house hidden beyond trees and fields with my view of the barns and all its animals that laze about on this cold, crisp, Autumn morning. The old bus makes its difficult, but necessary three-point turn on the narrow dirt road because this is the end of the line, the end of the road down in this hidden valley that lies at the bottom of this craggy old mountain. The driver does this with ease as she has been driving this route to my house for some years now. She readies the cranky old bus to begin by bringing it up to speed to match the far-reaching and very steep hill It must climb to get out of here and onto school some eight miles away. With the pedal to the metal, we're off like a cannon! We go up the hill like a champion and on further still to pick up everyone else and get on with another day of learning.

Two old buses pull into Center Elementary School in Westhampton, Massachusetts. They come from each side of the widespread Hilltown, it's hard to imagine nowadays, but the entire first through sixth grade fits into these two buses. It's hard to imagine as well that such a place could exist within deep hills, vast farmland, and dense forests so far away from homes where fires burn to warm their houses and live simple lives of disconnect and peaceful existence. That was what it was like back in 1978. Here rests a story of truth about how I lived in a small town, in a small school, with only thirteen students in fourth grade.

The buses are now parked on the cracked and slightly heaved blacktop, kids begin to file off to here and there, like ants on a mission to save their colonies. The schoolyard fills up in a matter of minutes and there's a lot of yelling and running about. The Bell rings for the day to start at 9:00 AM. The day moves on and into my trepid education. I sit in the front row of class, directly in front of Mrs. Piper's desk. I am feeling displaced and not particularly happy about it. You see I'm a talker, I talk, morning, noon, and night. Mrs. Piper has had enough of chiding me to stop talking and being disruptive during class, so here I sit writing on my bright yellow lined paper, *I will not talk in class* on every line of its demanding space. Why can't I just be good and quiet? What's wrong with me? I just can't seem to help it. When something interesting or funny comes to mind, I feel compelled to share it with my friends. Mrs. Piper doesn't think so though, she says, "Save it for recess, Julia, save it for after school!"

I think she just doesn't understand what it's like where I live, I live so very far away, from here, from my friends, no one wants to come to play at my house, their parents say, "It's too far back on those old dirt roads, it is too deep in the woods next to that scary looking mountain!" I find myself daydreaming about my animal friends that live in the big barns and fields around my house, they listen to me, they care. I'm always hopeful that one day, magically, one of them will talk back to me! Breaking my wandering thoughts as the day is nearing to end and the three o'clock Bell is ticking closer, Mrs. Piper says, "It's free time, but not for you, Julia, you need to finish your assignment." The life-changing Bell is about to ring which will release us to the veil of deep country life, but here I sit writing, and writing, I want to be with my friends shuffling about, talking in small groups, whispering about weekend plans, where we will go, plans for city trips, or necessary grocery shopping with mothers. Here I sit sullen, my punishment is to silence me, make me have some control, I become lost in my self-pity.

I hear a symphony of scuttling, squeaky tennis shoes on the linoleum floor, desks and chairs being pushed out of the way with an urgency to match. My classmates have perched themselves by the near floor-to-ceiling windows that look out onto the schoolyard where the buses sit waiting for the final release of the day. "There's a man on a horse!" calls out Linda. Another student yells out, "Julia, I think it's your father!" I look over to the kids and out the window to see a young man in his late twenties perched atop a speckled Brown and White Horse.

"That is my father," I say flatly. Excitement is brewing in my small class, there are giggles, oohs, ahs, and oh wows heard. The kids were enjoying the new, something, so different to happen at school, at the end of the day, in the small town that is so very far removed, as busy cities, such as Northampton, or Amherst seem so far away.

"Julia, I guess you won't be riding the bus today!" exclaims, Linda.

I smile and respond, "Nope, not today." The kids laugh and poke fun at the thought of riding a horse home, perhaps if it was the 1870s, it would be common of course to ride a horse home from school, but here we are in 1978, and I'll tell you, I think it's great!

The bell finally rings, and I have my complete sheet of paper filled written lines of teacher-bearing redemption. I lay it on Mrs. Piper's desk, then quickly rummaged through my own desk and find two books that I think I must take home. One is *The Adventures of Pippi Long Stocking's,* the other a short biography of Abraham Lincoln, whom I am fascinated by these days. My classroom is filled with chatter and joy because we are about to leave out the door, and run down the hall to the front doors, which are held open by two teachers. We file out in a disorganized fashion and head for the two buses waiting for our arrival, save me, Julia, from Morin Hollow, the girl who lives at the foot of a giant Mountain so far away from school, and very far away from a more civilized world.

I walk to my father who greets me with a fine, hello! He dismounts off the back of his brown and white speckled, Appaloosa horse, Cinnamon. I hand him my two most coveted books which he places in a small bag attached to her saddle. My father picks me up easily, as I am feather-light and small as a squirrel. He places me behind the saddle on Cinnamons ample and silken soft rump. I feel quite comfortable here as she is kind, and a gentle Mare too. She's very large, sixteen hands or so, with deep amber eyes that have the confidence of the strongest of men.

She is my father's horse, therefore, I believe that she is so strong, and so confident because he also, is. She is a reflection into my father's soul and mind. At this time, the two old yellow buses have fired up again and begin to amble off from the old Center School at the end of the day in an old Massachusetts Hilltown, far away from the cities below. I can hear the bus's engines fade off, and they're out of sight. My father hoists himself up and places himself expertly in the saddle in front of me, careful not to knock me back. Now we are off, clip, clopping our way over the cracked and slightly heaved blacktop, and on to the soft side of the road. I listen to the rhythmic creaking of the saddle as Cinnamon's big hips move side to side with each leg stride. We don't talk much for a while, we just drink it in, all the birds singing and chirping in the midafternoon light. I look down and watch the careful steps of Cinnamon's hooves. I see leaves and sticks, a bug here and there. I've become tired as the ride becomes almost hypnotic and quieting to my mind. I lean forward and lay my head on my father's back and close my eyes for a little while. It's so nice to be here in this space and time, how lucky I am.

The afternoon light is fading, the forest colors take on shadows that play and dance on rocks under the trees light, wind blows through and makes the colorful leaves of red, orange, and browns jump into little spiraling whirls that bounce around the forest floor. We move through at a nice rocking pace. My father has now begun to move Cinnamon off the gravel road and into the woods and onto an old dirt road named, Old Kings Highway Road, a very long, but often forgotten and rarely used road that used to be one of the main ways to go from Boston to the mountains of the Berkshires, then onto, Albany New York. It is a narrow, softly packed dirt road that curves and winds through the very old and dense forests that have steep hills to climb with guardrail-less cliffs on its sides at times. Cars would find it difficult to use, buses surely would not, but we would ride on unencumbered by anything with us perched atop this loving and peaceful horse. I do believe Cinnamon also enjoyed our journey back home, to the farm, and the life that we lived as a group, but as one, too.

We were more than halfway home on this beautiful Autumn Day in October of 1978, peacefully moving and being content with life, when suddenly a car engine ignited with a roar and the defiance of a rebellion! We couldn't see the car, but it was dangerously close by, too close. To our immediate right, lurching from the far side of very large stack of cut timber logs, a black car screeches its tires, its engine roars, a sound so loud it hurts my ears, the car lurches towards us, its back tires sliding sideways, soft plumes of dust spit out from each side of its tires. I tense up and grab the back of the saddle with fright. Cinnamon knew that the steep and rocky embankment was there next to her, my father too, I didn't see it, but there we were. At this moment, Cinnamon side stepped to move away from the demonizing car, and that sidestep took us down the loose embankment, her heavy body pulling us over, but then she collapsed down onto her legs. We begin to slide backwards, and down the loose embankment, nearly at a straight up and down angle. I hear my father yell, "hold on!" I feel my legs go back behind me, but I am held up by the back of Cinnamons big, and powerful legs, my tiny hands are gripped like a vice to the saddleback, my face pressed into the love of her strong, but soft body. I feel her throughout my entire torso, even her tail is touching me. We slid down the bank five, ten, twenty feet, as if we were on a slide in a City Park. I see Cinnamon's hooves are pressing hard like you would on a brake pedal, forcing a stop, and she does. As quickly as we went down, she dug in deep to the Cliffside, and bravely she brought us back up to the top of the road. Just like that, we were safe, we lived, we were unscathed and uninjured, my father and me.

Here I find myself cleaved to the saddle with my tiny little hands, I realize I can let go now, and I do, I land smartly on my feet. My father dismounts as well.

I don't remember the words we spoke to each other that day in the middle of the woods, more than halfway back to our farm in 1978, but I do remember this, Cinnamon craned her neck upwards and let out a high whinnying bellow, she gave herself a nice shake, like a dog that's been out in the rain, then gave a shutter, then peacefully relaxes as she once was before we fell off the side of the road. My father looks up and down at each of her legs, checks for any cuts or injuries and finds only a very small scratch. He picks me up, places me on Cinnamon's ample and soft rump, mounts up himself, and we move on, as we know, and have always known, trust is love. My father says, "let's go." Cinnamon steps up, and we ride off into the woods once again, peacefully, and truthfully at home.

The Walk

It was a Monday morning with rain that just started pebbling in at a slant, cold and sharp, the kind that stings on warm skin. Layla had found herself walking on a dirt path leading up to a soggy hill near the edge of town, near the edge of a lake. She is on her way to see about a job. It's been her conviction to get her self-employed, save money, and get herself out of these hills with old faces. Layla, a girl of nineteen is not particularly attractive, but amiably well received in her little village town. She happens to be walking here when she comes upon a sitting man, cross-legged and perched at the top of a large boulder. He is still, but not ominously bothered by Layla's appearance. "Are you a lost girl?" Asks the sitting man. Layla bends her neck upwards to meet his questioning eyes, water drips from the brim of her hooded hat, and falls to her mouth, one drop clings to her bottom lip like a tear daring to the fall. "I, no, no I'm not lost." Replies Layla. The sitting man holds up his hands, palms open, as if he were holding back traffic for her to pass. Layla nods her head and with a wave of her hand, walks on. Layla scans her surroundings and presses on away from the sitting man. That man was out in the woods, perched as he was upon a rock did not concern her, but she noted he hadn't had any hat or coat to protect himself from the elements, and this worried her.

The rain had already been soaking through her yellow slicker, but she is warm inside its plastic cocoon. Layla thought to herself that life has been an insurmountable compilation of misfortunate events. As an infant, the first was when she had been dumped off on the un-mowed lawn of a poor old woman. Layla had laid there for many hours unnoticed and untouched till a curious dog found her, then barked and howled incessantly. Curious enough that is how she was given her name by the poor old woman; it was her **dog** that was named Layla. She was a very kind, and exceptionally motherly White German Shepherd. She was the best of caretakers for humans and animals alike. She was known to nurse a few kittens alongside of her puppies, and watch over the poor old woman, too.

Layla shakes her head and her mind a bit trying to clear it. She pursues to focus on the path ahead of her. She walks deeper and deeper into the woods. Now, the rain falls with more of a purpose, big heavy drops descend with force and begin to sting like needles on her face. She starts to shiver, all around her little rivulets of streams begin to flow with intent down the wild wooded path, carrying with it little stones and fragmented leaves flowing effortlessly. Now begins Layla's test to become stronger than her past that has forsaken her for a destiny she can let go of now.

With each step, it becomes more difficult to stay upright on the sloppy hill, as she comes to a corner that banks a hard right, looming nearby is a hung Cliffside, Layla slips and begins to slide down it, her shoes have become gum muddy, then come out from underneath her, she falls hard and begins to be pulled swiftly down to a looming edge, mud, leaves, and forest debris scratching her body as she slides down, and further down still.

The man who has been sitting tirelessly for hours was moved, too. Perhaps, it is either the torrid rain or sheer loneliness of his meditative rock that he now stands, stretches his limbs which extend to great lengths at all angles that he feels compelled to move. He appears slim and fit, he wears little clothing save for a faded pair of tight Jean shorts with a loosely fitted long sleeve shirt, the one perhaps someone would buy at a Rock Concert, its slacked sleeves hang dripping at the cuffs, the letters of a band name roughly seen on his chest read, Roll Stone, the wet of it sucks closely to his skin. He bends slightly and jumps from his perched place, once on the ground, his body looms gravely tall against the trees and shrubs around him. He rubs his cool face and runs a hand over his short gray hair, he is overcome with the need to move for what no one knows.

He starts down onto the path that Layla used just a short time ago. Trudging through mud and water, the rain beats against his thin unwavering body as he easily glides through the storm, he is not unencumbered at all by the onslaught of this torrid weather, barefooted, he steps and mud squelches, squirms, and slides under his feet, but it does not slow his pace, he is deliberate and infiltrating, he walks on and through.

The rain begins to wane a bit, ever so slightly at first, then its heaviness changes to just a pattering shower. The rain is gentler and fluid warm, but darkness grows near. Layla after being hurled mercilessly over and off the path is now straddling the cliff that she is cleaved to by her tiny hands at the edge of an outcropping, holding on to its dirty roots, feet dangling, arms crimped into its routed ledge. Layla waits for what she knows to be, none other than she has always known, which is a compilation of unfortunate events, but she's not letting go.

The sitting man is dangerously close now to coming upon the place that Layla has so quickly veered off from. He slows his stride as he begins to descend the hill that the rains have washed out, and the once well-marked path is now cavernous and jagged. The man must sidestep his way down, he appears as if he were on a sheet of ice and a fall would be tragic, at any moment he could lose his footing. Perhaps from his enormous height, the world appears so very far down, he might have a story to tell, but no one knows. The air has become thick with moisture, so thick that heavy fog moves in, and over the hill, next to the lake, by the little town that not a particularly attractive girl, clings to by her meager, jobless life, with her small hands at the edge of a path, well washed out from a hard rain that fell.

As the mountainous, large, and tall, once sitting man reaches the precipice on this jagged path down, he stops ever so smartly, and at this moment, at this very instance, he stands dead still, so still he could feel his exaggerated heartbeat in his ears, pounding. There is the faintest of sound in the air, almost a purr, but more like hummingbird wings flapping ever so peacefully in his ear. The once sitting man at this moment closes his eyes and appreciates the beautiful sound he hears and imagines the beauty of the world in all things possible.

Standing tall over the cliff which Layla cleaves to with all her life, he opens his eyes and looks down into Layla's and gently asks ever so honestly, "Are you a lost girl here?" Layla, being so stuck, and so caught in the roots and sharp edges of the steep cliffside, replies, "Yes I was."

The once sitting man extends his long arm, and warm heart to Layla, "Take my hand, your life is about to change."

"The greatest thing you'll ever learn is
just to love and be loved in return."

Eden Ahbez

Their Story – Summer 1965

You could hear the summer crickets playing their song with the cicadas in a pitched symphony that night. It covered the sound of the heavy tires that crunched in the driveway's dirt. The 1960 powder blue and silver Chevy convertible rolled out as quietly as it could have passed the lighted window where Margaret Warner sat at her kitchen table reading her newspaper.

Three young teenagers pushed the heavy car down the driveway, they were crouched at its sides. One teenager with the door propped open holding the steering wheel straight. The car rolls out nicely past the two-story colonial house, some of its occupants sound asleep inside, except for Margaret who sits illuminated by the window light. Ellie looks over at her mother. She winces a little and feels a slight ping of guilt for sneaking her mother's car out with her boyfriend Dave and his friend Bob tonight but, roll on they do down the driveway and out onto the street.

Bob, a gangly looking teenager with dark hair and eyes to match, says, "Let me drive, Ellie."

She tosses him the keys. She had so giftedly lifted it from her mother's pocketbook earlier that evening. "Drive slow," she says.

The three teenagers pop themselves in the car, one, two, three. Bob behind the wheel, Ellie in the middle, and Dave beside her in the passenger seat. The doors shut with a careful click, Bob puts the key in the ignition the powder blue and silver Chevy fires right up. With their hearts pumping at a fast clip and adrenaline coursing through their young bodies. They drive off down the unlit street some twenty feet or so, Ellie reaches past Bob's hands on the steering wheel and pulls a silver knob on the dashboard, turning on the headlights. Just then, another car pulls out of a side street nearly clipping the back end of the convertible. The driver honks his horn and shouts out his window, "Hey!" Bob hits his gas pedal with a punch. The big Chevy speeds off down the street. They laugh and are feeling elated now that they have pulled off the grand car theft.

"Let's put the top down on this convertible," says Bob.

"Nah, it's better if we leave it up, we did borrow the car without asking, we don't want someone to spot us," replies Dave.

"Exactly," says Ellie.

Ellie and Dave sit close together. Dave holds her hand and gives a slight squeeze as if to say...

Dave and Ellie are THAT couple, the couple that are both so good-looking, it hurts your eyes to look at them, they are THAT couple that has been marked in high school as most beautiful, most popular. Dave with his mysterious hazel eyes and handsomely chiseled face, light brown hair sharp in a Marine Corp cut, high and tight! Ellie, the picture of beauty with soft brown eyes, dark auburn hair that rolls down her back with a face of a gilded Renoir.

The three teenagers are thoroughly enjoying their ride around town, further accelerating it with a song "Drive my car" by The Beatles, playing loudly. This is the crowd in the new kids of 1965. No broken hearts here. The kids sing along "Baby you can drive my car, and maybe I love you" are the last and resonating lyrics they will hear that night on their joy-filled ride of youth that lets them feel as if they are invincible and will yield to no one, not even themselves. Darkness creeps in the new Chevy convertible, the dash lights set a glow on the kids' youth, smiles abound and freedom reigns, giving them a euphoric view of life not yet lived to see around the corner with experience. A corner it was, heavy on tires thick with a rubber sole, sliding on slippery gravel too fast too hard, one flip, two flips, three flips, telephone pole. House lights go off one by one, down the street and onto the next block and on through the small city. Streetlights clip off one after the other.

The moon and starlight are all that breathe life into them now. And breathe they do. They walk away. A bit dazed, bumped and scratched, not so much for the heap of scrap metal that used to be a fine car. Northampton, Massachusetts spent a dark night that evening in 1965. Dave and Ellie head off down a set of railroad tracks nearby. Bob runs away down the street into the night and with his teenage years ticking down like a stopwatch, but not in minutes or hours, but a three-year plan instead.

A few walking miles of near silence, the young couple cannot imagine a fate less than the totaled car they left behind. Near Ellie's house, they stop off at her friend, Nancy's house, who is camping out in her backyard with a couple of other classmates. There is a campfire ablaze with the smell of burnt pine and maple, it draws Ellie and Dave closer. They talk it over with their confidants about the accident.

"What happens next?" says Ellie.

"We tell the truth," responds Dave.

"My mother is going to kill me."

"Let's get this over with," says Dave.

The kids say their goodbyes there are 'well wishes' and 'it is going to be 'oks' heard.

Would it though?

What could possibly be the punishment for Ellie and Dave? The two teenagers walk up the backyard between Ellie's house and a neighbors. Quietly, they stand in the shadows out by the back garage some distance from the house. They notice flashlights bobbing here and there in it as well as a shiny police car in the driveway. Accompanied by Dave's father's station wagon.

"Oh no," says Ellie.

"Shit is going to get real," says Dave.

Hand in hand they walk forward to find out their fate, facing it head-on. Instead of from the side like that destroyed car they left behind. The side impact of the telephone poll and keeping the top on of that convertible saved them that night. Seatbelts? The car did not even have them. With foot-tapping Margaret, Ellie's mother stands in the doorway as the couple approach, "Call your father at the Longmeadow house, he has a few words for you." Dave's parents stand shaking their heads, the rest is history for them.

Dave was sent to live in Vermont with his aunt Ginny and uncle Gerald, he would end up working on a dairy farm for the family and would go on fishing trips to Lake Champlain and hunting in the green mountains, he would end up loving his time here, and the family that became so very important to the young man he became. He missed Ellie of course.

That very cold and dissenting conversation Ellie had with her father that night in 1965 after the "accident" would leave Ellie sent off to an all-girls boarding school in Crafts bury, Vermont. Some 20 miles from the Canadian border, and more than 200 miles from Dave.

Dave's time away was about a year, Ellies time was also the year in penance, though, Dear Prudence was there, Ellie's roommate, she made the time a little better for her, Prudence was always so kind to her. She liked to burn incense and candles in their shared dorm room, and play new music records of the up and coming folk and rock bands. She was even known to sneak in a puppy or two. Just for the fun love of it. Prudence had a peaceful way about her, unassuming to anyone, especially Ellie.

Life would pass without any interruptions or visits home over the next year for Ellie. She was sixteen when she was finally allowed to go home, Dave too.

What will they do?

Find each other in high school hallways?

Perhaps cross each other's path on the city sidewalk?

See each other over a campfire out at a friend's house?

Maybe they meet each other behind an old house next to an old garage with a set of train tracks behind them near the center of town, that might lead them to times and years where there is another car accident, the Vietnam war, a baby girl is born, and perhaps as well a Beatles song that comes along too, that's part of Their story.

A Wayward Guest

I was living in Vermont, near the Canadian border with only about twenty girls at a private school. It turned out well enough, but by late spring we were told to go home and wait for a letter telling our parents the girls' school would move to a new location in Egremont, Massachusetts and with directions on how to get there as well. When summer came and the letter arrived, only ten of us showed up to the new school a week before Labor Day, but the school would only last until December, closing for good.

It is fall of 1965 in a small Massachusetts town beneath the foothills of the Berkshire Mountains in the new school of only ten girls, living in a clean, but barely renovated 18th century Inn. There was also an old barn behind it as well where one of the girls kept a horse. We had four classes of English, Math, World History, and Spanish, taught by three teachers. A married couple from Argentina and a Spanish man from Spain too, living all together under one big roof. This school started the year before as an unsuccessful attempt to make it Coed with the boy's school nearby in Great Barrington.

Here begins my recollection of one very strange experience in that house. One weekend, I stayed behind while most of the girls and teachers went off into town for errands and shopping. I had decided that morning to investigate the part of the Inn which was off-limits. The third floor, I was told not to go there because it was unused, kept closed for a very long time and that it was more like an attic.

One late evening after a few weeks of living here, I thought it odd to hear footsteps on the floor above me as I lay in my bed, I thought why were the girls up there and why didn't they invite me with them? I wondered enviously what a great adventure they were having, especially after last call, sneaking their way through the long and twisting hallways up there, breaking the rules right under the noses of the teachers. Wasn't the door locked? I passed by it a few times thinking, what was up there? This morning, I found it is not locked now. I was anxious to see for myself, after all, how could they not ask me to come with them last night since I was a popular girl here wasn't I? I will go and explore it myself; I will go and take in every detail I find, maybe even Snoop through things they missed, and then wish they had, and I wouldn't say a word until I hear about their own mystery tour. I was going to go up there as the morning light crept in and everyone else in the house was in town now. I set off to explore the 3rd floor of this ancient Inn. I was a bit nervous as I made my way towards the door listening for the slightest sound of anyone coming. I reached the door and hesitated a bit, then I turned the antique doorknob carefully not to make any sound, it groaned then clicked quietly as it opened. A stale and dry dusty smell greets me at the bottom step, a sliver of light bounces down the narrow wooden steps before me. What will I find, and what will I do if I find something I shouldn't?

The door was open and my daring exploring set to begin. I hesitated for a moment, dismissed my fear, and ascended the steep captain's ship stairs, narrow at the step and tight as a drum. I stand in absolute awe at the top of the floor. I stood there for several minutes unsure if I should turn and go back. My eyes scan the distance from side to side through its tunnel-like hall, with doors that must lead into rooms on both sides. I felt like I was in the Twilight zone, all appeared dark and Gray with barely a sliver of light across the floor from a window somewhere here.

I decided I must move from my spot. My breathing was slow, and my heart was quick as I started to walk slowly, almost on tiptoes in my brown leather penny loafers against the wide wood plank floors. My eyes opened wider as I took in the scene before me; should I keep going, I think to myself? I approach the first room and find myself inside, "There!" I say, that's not so bad, relax, my heart stopped racing a bit, as I looked around in a small room. How odd this room looks, old things are spaced sparingly apart, with a few pieces of very old furniture, it looked as though someone had lived here, but had left everything as it was, back in time. I moved on to another tiny narrow hallway, leading to another door that was half open. Within the room it led somewhere else, but I did not go into that next room. I looked for a light switch, but there were none to be found, and not a lamp either. I went back into the first long hallway to possibly venture further, but I became overwhelmed of where to go next. I was aware that my bravery was waning, as my blood was pumping through every vein, hard and fast.

I stood facing toward the other rooms ahead, but I couldn't seem to make out where they ended. It looked to be a short distance at the start, maybe there's a door down the end of it? I walked on further down the shadowy hall to find yet another set of doors on the left and right of me, opening the one on my left. I began walking into this room, but suddenly it appeared very far away, and the walls seemed to be moving like one breathing in and out. I was really trying to push myself to go on, one step then another, but were my feet really moving? I looked down; I was still standing where I was before. Now what I asked myself was, should I go on? Then I heard a distant sound, a kind of rustling, I think. It must be from behind me because I saw nothing in front of me, so I looked around, nothing there. I heard it again, this time it was so close; it felt like a coldness went right through me. At that moment, the whole place feels like ice, so cold that I felt the hair on my arms stand up!

Then the sound I heard was a woman's voice, sighing, not a sad sigh, but a disgusted sigh.

OK! Whatever is going on, it isn't supposed to be happening. I felt as though I levitated off the floor, with a single twist in midair I shot as an arrow would down the hallway to the stairs that led to the second floor. I went down in a flash! I slammed the door behind me as I kept running to my room. When I felt myself enter back into the reality of where I was on the second floor, I shook from my head to my toes!

Years later I said to myself, I only imagined all that, it never happened, better to forget it; that year in 1965 at Mount Everett Preparatory School for Girls. Incredibly, I did manage to forget this supernatural occurrence for some time. I wished for many things in my life to distract me from my unwanted memories and as it turned out, what I remembered all these years later was that not one student that I lived with there, at that old Inn, ever admitted she had been up there, on the third floor. I did find out that in the early 1970s the Inn had burned to the ground from a lightning strike during a late summer storm. It was said to be a complete inferno that started on the third floor and burned the entire Inn to the ground quickly, and then left it a pile of ash and copper colored smoke rising. I never told anyone my story till now about the sighing lady, the Wayward Guest.

CPSIA information can be obtained
at www.ICGtesting.com
Printed in the USA
BVHW042059290322
632756BV00012B/274

9 781649 796394